DANNY'S DOODLES

The Squirting Donuts

DANNY'S DOODLES

The Squirting Donuts

Story and illustrations by
David A. Adler

sourcebooks
jabberwocky

Published by Sourcebooks Jabberwocky, an imprint of Sourcebooks, Inc.
P.O. Box 4410, Naperville, Illinois 60567-4410
(630) 961-3900
Fax: (630) 961-2168   9-14
www.jabberwockykids.com

Library of Congress Cataloging-in-Publication data is on file with the publisher.

Source of Production: Bang Printing, Brainerd, Minnesota, USA
Date of Production: August 2014
Hardcover Run Number: 5002033
Trade Paperback Run Number: 5002028

Printed and bound in the United States of America.
BG 10 9 8 7 6 5 4 3 2 1

For my ever-lovely wife Renée

Contents

Chapter 1

MARSHMALLOW ON WHOLE WHEAT

I'm warning you. I'm about to say two mean and nasty words.

If I say them at school, kids shudder and run away. If I say them at home, my sister Karen says I should be punished for talking dirty.

Are you ready?

Here are the two words:

Mrs. Cakel.

She's my teacher and she's super mean and nasty. She makes lunch checks. She won't let any of us have soda, hard candy, cherries, or pomegranate juice. She says that's so we eat nutritious lunches and don't get red stains on our clothes.

She won't let Annie Abrams wear her favorite yellow headband.

"It's not becoming," she told Annie.

There are so many rules in our class that my friend Calvin Waffle tells me, "It's lucky she lets us breathe." But he doesn't tell that to Mrs. Cakel. You can't tell her anything.

Everyone is afraid of her.

At parent-teacher conferences—you know, when the teacher tells parents what's wrong with their kids—she told my mother not to slouch, to sit up straight. She told her not to mumble. And do you know what? Mom sat up and spoke up. And Mom is not a fourth-grade student. She's a chemical engineer. I don't know exactly what she does, just that she works in a laboratory and has to wear a large white coat.

Dad was also at school that night.

"I didn't talk to your teacher. I didn't ask her anything," Dad told me later. "I was afraid to."

I tell you. Everyone is afraid of that woman. Once our principal, Mr. Telfer, walked into class and he was chewing gum. It was a medicated gum to help him stop smoking. Mrs. Cakel pointed to the big NO sign that lists all the things we're not allowed to do in our class.

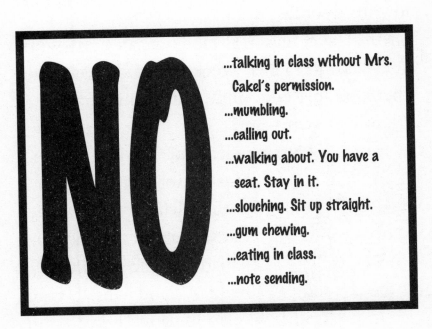

NO

...talking in class without Mrs. Cakel's permission.

...mumbling.

...calling out.

...walking about. You have a seat. Stay in it.

...slouching. Sit up straight.

...gum chewing.

...eating in class.

...note sending.

Then she held a garbage can under Mr. Telfer's chin and made him spit out the gum. She did that in front of our entire class.

And he's the principal!

It's Monday morning. I sit by my desk and copy the work on the board. It's easy. When it's done, I doodle. That's what I do when I'm bored. That's pretty much what I always do. I love to doodle.

Mrs. Cakel tells us to take out our homework. We had lots this weekend and now she's checking it. I take mine out of my book bag.

Jason's Lawn Care?

Spring cleanup???

This is not my homework. It's the bill from the gardener.

I think about this morning. I had Sugar Flakes for breakfast and they tasted like toothpaste. I *was* tasting toothpaste. I hadn't rinsed enough when I brushed my teeth so I went back to the bathroom, only Karen was in there. I think she does her homework in the bathroom, or tries to make herself look normal, or something that could take forever.

I waited.

She finally came out, smiled, patted her hair, and went downstairs.

I went in, rinsed, and rushed to eat the flakes that no longer tasted like toothpaste but were really soggy. I grabbed my homework and my lunch and hurried out.

My lunch!

I reach in my desk, take out my lunch bag, and look inside. Lipstick? Mineral body lotion? Face powder? Eyeliner? What is this stuff? Where are my sandwich, pretzels, and apple?

This morning I took all the wrong stuff. I bet right now Mom is sending my homework to the gardener and putting my sandwich in the medicine cabinet.

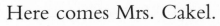

Here comes Mrs. Cakel.

She'll get bogey-eyed when I tell her I don't have my homework. She'll make me copy all the *H* and *W* words in the dictionary.

"*H* and *W* are for homework," she'll tell me. "Once you copy those words maybe you'll remember to do yours."

She'll make me stay in class during lunch and do my homework, and the worst part is, she'll be in the room with me. How could I eat looking at her? I'll lose my appetite.

Oh! That's right. I don't have a lunch. All I have is lipstick, lotion, powder, and eyeliner.

She stands by my desk.

"I did my homework," I say, "but I left it at home."

"Bring it in tomorrow," she says and walks to Greg. He sits behind me.

Huh? Who said that?

It gets worse, or better. I'm not sure if it's good or bad when Mrs. Cakel is nice. I'm not sure it's Mrs. Cakel.

She is teaching us about the American Revolution—you know, when George Washington and the Continental Army fought the British. She asks my friend Calvin Waffle, "Who fired the first shots at Lexington and Concord?"

"Not me," Calvin answers. "I don't even have a gun."

That's it, I think. *She's going to explode.*

The Great WAFFLE!

I hold my hands over my ears. But she doesn't yell. She just calls on my friend Douglas Miller and asks him.

"The British fired the first shots," Douglas answers. "They had lots of guns and fancy red uniforms."

I must be in some alternate universe. Up is down. Big is small. Vinegar is sweet and so is Mrs. Cakel.

I'm right-handed, so I try doodling with my left hand. It comes out as just scribbles. If I was in a true alternate universe, my left-hand doodles would look to me like my right-hand doodles. I look up. There it is: the ceiling. In an alternate universe, I would look up and see the floor. I'm not the one in an alternate universe. Mrs. Cakel is.

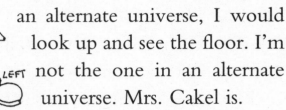

Now, I bet, when she looks in a mirror, she sees Mrs. Herman, my kindergarten teacher. Nothing ever upset Mrs. Herman.

The bell rings. It's time for lunch. I buy a container of milk. Then I tell Calvin, Annie, and Douglas about

8

my lunch of lipstick, lotion, powder, and eyeliner, and they each give me something to eat.

Annie gives me celery sticks. Douglas gives me some of his pressed fruit roll. And Calvin gives me half of his marshmallow-banana-carrot-on-whole-wheat-bread sandwich.

DOUGLAS

I look at the whole wheat with white marshmallow ooze dripping out.

"Do you like this stuff?" I ask.

Calvin shakes his head. He doesn't.

"Why don't you ask your mother to make you something else for lunch?"

ANNIE

"She doesn't make my lunch," he answers. "I do."

I wonder why Calvin would make a lunch for himself that he knows he won't like. There's probably no good answer to that question. It's just hard to explain Calvin Waffle.

9

I bite into the sandwich. The marshmallow and banana are sweet. The carrots give it a crispy crunch. Those parts are good, but I don't like the bread.

I try not to think about what I'm eating. I think about Mrs. Cakel.

"Something is wrong," I say. "Something is bothering Mrs. Cakel."

"Yeah, she's all sweet and lovey," Douglas says. "She's acting like Mrs. Herman."

Calvin doesn't know about Mrs. Herman. He just moved here with his mother. He told me his father is on some spying mission. That's right. He says his father is a spy, but I'm not sure that's true.

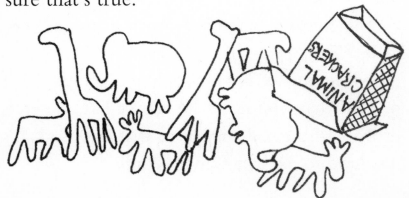

Douglas tells Calvin about Mrs. Herman.

"She gave us animal crackers for snack, and the first time I got a horse cracker, I threw it on the floor and stepped on it. I didn't like horses."

"You also stepped on the moose," Annie says.

"That's because I thought they were horses with horns."

"And do you know what Mrs. Herman did?" Douglas asked.

Calvin shook his head. He didn't know.

"She hugged me and said she was sorry. And from then on, she made sure I never got a horse cookie for snack."

"Now Mrs. Cakel is acting like that," I say, "and it's not normal."

"Maybe it's not really her," Annie says. "Maybe she's her twin sister. Maybe the two of them are exactly the same but opposite. Maybe they're mirror twins."

"No, it's her," Douglas says. "She knows all our names. She knows all those things about

George Washington, that his father's name was Augustine and his mother's was Mary. She knows all about his wife and his stepchildren. Only a real teacher knows that stuff."

"I'm used to the old Mrs. Cakel," I say. "We've got to get back our mean and nasty teacher."

"Why?" Calvin asks.

"Yeah, why?" Annie says. "She's being nice. Teachers should be nice."

I take another bite of my Calvin sandwich. I get mostly bread and marshmallow.

Annie chews her noisy celery.

"Maybe she'll suddenly explode," Douglas says, spinning his apple on the table. "Maybe all this nice stuff will be too much for her."

Calvin has a rice cake in a small plastic sandwich bag for dessert. He puts it flat on the table, punches it again and again until it's a bag of rice crumbs. Then he pours the crumbs into his mouth.

"You're right," Annie says. "Something is wrong with Mrs. Cakel. Maybe we should help her, but not right now. First let's enjoy a vacation from mean."

Calvin brushes rice cake crumbs off his shirt and pants.

"We could slouch, mumble, and send notes," Douglas says, "but I still can't chew gum. My dentist says that's bad for my teeth."

"It would be nice not to have so many rules," I say, "but what will happen to her nickname 'No, No, No Cakel'?"

"We could call her 'Chew, Chew Cakel,' or 'Mumble, Bumble Cakel,'" Calvin says. "We could call her whatever we want and she'll just say, 'That's nice.'"

"No," Annie says and shakes her head. "We've got to help that woman."

"Yes!" Calvin says a bit too loud.

13

He stands, points to the cafeteria ceiling, and declares, "This calls for the Great Waffle!"

Douglas says, "I want mine with maple syrup."

"I'm not joking," Calvin says and sits down. "We can't help her until we find out what's wrong, and for that we'll have to do some spy work. And I'm the one who knows about spy work."

He smiles.

"But before we help her," Calvin says, "I'll have some fun. This afternoon I'm going to see how many of Cakel's No things I can get away with."

On our way back to class, I try to talk Calvin out of his plan to send notes, mumble, chew gum, and whatever. But he just smiles and walks ahead.

When I get to class, Calvin is already there. He's walking about and mumbling. Mrs. Cakel is sitting by her desk and guess what? She's slouching.

I sit in my seat and watch the two of them.

Mrs. Cakel doesn't seem to notice Calvin. She doesn't seem to notice any of us.

Calvin sits in his seat and slouches.

Mrs. Cakel doesn't react.

Calvin stands on his seat and pretends to be chewing gum.

Mrs. Cakel still sits there.

Calvin tears paper from his spiral notebook, scribbles something on it, folds it into an airplane, and sends it to me.

I unfold the airplane.

"Who is that woman?" Calvin wrote.

I look at her. She has that blank stare look, you know, like she doesn't see anything even if it's right in front of her.

Something is wrong. Something is terribly wrong.

Chapter 2

THE JELLY HYPODERMIC

"Do you know where she lives?" Calvin asks on our way home.

Calvin and I live on the same block so we walk together to and from school.

I shake my head. I don't know where Mrs. Cakel lives.

"That won't stop us," Calvin says. "We'll find her. My father taught me lots of spy tricks."

Calvin says his father speaks lots of languages and that right now he is on a secret spy mission for our government. Calvin's mom told me his dad is a truck driver and one day he went across the state to deliver some furniture and never came back.

I asked Calvin if that was true.

"That's Dad's cover," Calvin said. "We say he's a truck driver so no one will know what he really does."

If his being a spy is such a secret, why did he tell me?

Calvin says, "We can look on the Internet for Mrs. Cakel's address."

"She may not be listed."

"We can ask the principal, Mr. Telfer. I don't think he likes her."

"He won't give us a teacher's address."

"Then I'll use a spy trick." He leans close and whispers, "We'll put a tracking device in her book bag."

18

I look around. There is no one nearby.

"Why are you whispering?"

"The trees have ears," he whispers. This time his voice is even lower. "The sidewalk, street signs, and flowers have ears."

That's a lot of ears.

"This would be a homemade device," Calvin whispers. "We'll fill her book bag with tiny bread crumbs and poke a hole in the bottom of the bag. Then all we have to do is follow the crumby trail."

I look at Calvin.

He's serious.

"That's a Hansel and Gretel device," I say. "And anyway, she drives to school. There would be no trail. The crumbs would be on the floor of her car."

"Oh."

We are already on our block, just a few houses away from Calvin's.

"Why don't we just ask my sister where

Mrs. Cakel lives? Karen knows lots of personal stuff about our teachers."

Calvin's mom is standing in front of his house. At first she just waves to us. Then she jumps and waves.

GRRR!

GRRR!

GRRR!

She's really skinny and has long, curly red hair that is flying up and down. Her pants and shirt have lots of colored stripes and dots. When she jumps, all those colors mix and she looks like a broken kaleidoscope.

"Hurry! Hurry!" she shouts. "I have something to tell you."

We hurry to Calvin's front walk.

"What do I love more than anything?" Calvin's mother asks.

"Me," Calvin answers.

"Sure. But what do I love to do more than anything?"

"Word scrambles."

"Yeah. Here's a good one. V-F-W-A-L-L-I-N-F-A-C-E. What's that? And what's N-O-A-N-Y-C-H-E-N-D?"

She talks real slow now and loud and spells out those wacky words letter by letter.

Calvin and I shake our heads. We don't know what V-F-W-A-L-L-I-N-F-A-C-E and N-O-A-N-Y-C-H-E-N-D are.

Mrs. Waffle laughs and says, "That's you! I just mixed the letters in your names, Calvin Waffle and Danny Cohen. I'm surprised you didn't know that. You're both so young, and it's usually old people who forget their names, like the old man I was once sitting next to in a hotel lobby. I knew his name because it was on his luggage. Someone called out that his room was ready, and he just sat there. 'Don't you know your own name?' I asked him. 'My name? I don't even know your name,' he said."

"Mom," Calvin says. "You have something to tell me."

"Yes, when you get old, you should have a bracelet with your name on it so if you forget who you are, you can look at it and know."

"Mom, you were waving and jumping because you have something to tell me and I don't think it's to wear a bracelet."

"Was I waving? Oh, yes I was. I wanted to tell you about my new job at the bakery. You know I love to bake. I'll be baking bread and cake, and the best thing is I'll be using the hypodermic."

"The what?"

"You know, the needle. I'll be the one injecting donuts with jelly. I promise I'll bring some home for both of you with extra shots of jelly."

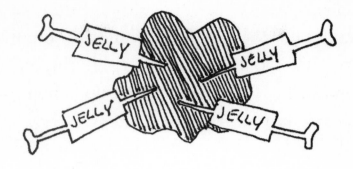

I love the jelly in those donuts. When I eat one, I always look for the side with the small hole. That's where most of the jelly is.

"That's great, Mom."

Calvin gives his mother his schoolbooks and tells her he's going to my house.

As we walk, I say, "Your mother is really lucky to have a job doing something she likes."

"She hasn't started," Calvin says. "Tomorrow she might come home covered with jelly and flour and complain that it's too hot with all those ovens on."

We're by my house. Calvin holds my books while I get my key out.

"She might say her boss is too grumpy or too bossy. Old people like my mother complain a lot. It's too hot. It's too cold. There's too much traffic. Prices keep going up. Their backs and legs hurt."

My mom and dad don't complain about all that stuff, and they certainly don't complain about their jobs. Dad actually says he likes what he does, and he sells plumbing supplies. How can anyone like selling pipes and plungers?

I open the door. Calvin gives me back my books and we walk in. Karen is in the kitchen having a snack. She has strange eating habits. She says, "You are what you eat," and right now she's a low-fat Greek yogurt.

Karen's school starts earlier in the morning and ends earlier in the afternoon than mine so that's why

MY SISTER KAREN

24

she's already home. She's in the eighth grade. That's almost high school.

"Something is going on with Dad," she says. "He came home a few minutes ago, went to his and Mom's room, and closed the door."

Dad is never home from work this early.

"And Mom called. She wants us to set the table and prepare dinner. We're eating at six."

Something is definitely going on. Mom almost never asks us to make dinner.

"I'll make salad," Karen says. "You'll make spaghetti, and we'll open a can of sauce."

Karen once filled a bowl with beans, chopped pickles and onions and tomato chunks, and called it a Health Salad. Well, it didn't do any good for my health. I didn't eat it and I don't think I'll eat the one she makes today. I'll just eat spaghetti.

I tell her about Mrs. Cakel.

"Are you sure it was her? Were you in the right room?"

"It was her," Calvin says, "and she was really nice. I don't think it's a problem but your brother is worried."

"Yeah, that's my brother. Danny is a real worrier."

"Do you know where she lives?" I ask.

"Sure. Clover Street. I'm not sure of the number but it's a small blue house."

I pass Clover Street on the way to the library. It's just a few blocks away.

"We'll go later," I tell Calvin, "after we do our homework."

First I have to find the homework that got mixed up with the gardener's bill and put it in my book bag. Tomorrow I have to show it to Mrs. Cakel. She may no longer be in a lovey-dovey mood.

My homework is on the small table in the hall.

My lunch is there too. I take the gardener's bill and the bag with Mom's lipstick, mineral body lotion, face powder, and eyeliner and put in on the table. I put the homework in my book bag.

Then I deal with my lunch.

I put my sandwich and apple in the refrigerator. I open the small bag of pretzels and share them with Calvin. Then we sit together by the kitchen table and do our homework.

Chapter 3

ADVENTURE ON CLOVER STREET

I tell Karen, "Calvin and I are going for a walk."

"To Clover Street?"

I nod.

"Don't let her see you. Teachers don't like kids to know where they live. And be back in an hour, in time to help me with dinner."

Before I leave the kitchen, Calvin gives me his homework. "Put this in your book bag," he says. "You can give it to me tomorrow in school."

I look at the top of his homework page. I want to be sure his name is on it. I don't want to mix his papers with mine. Trust me on this. You don't want to mix your work with Calvin's.

Last week one of our history questions was, "When was Benjamin Franklin born?" Calvin answered, "On his birthday."

"How much is 567 multiplied by 64?" was one of our math problems. "A lot," is what Calvin wrote. The real answer is 36,288. I'm good at math.

"Remember! Be back by five," Karen shouts as we leave.

"Where's Clover?" Calvin asks.

"It's close. I'll show you."

Calvin just moved here, so he doesn't know all the streets. I've met his mother lots of times. Calvin says I may have even met his father.

"Spies wear lots of disguises," he told me. "The man who cuts your hair may really be my dad."

"No," I said. "I've been going to the same barber for lots of years."

"He could be your bus driver."

"I don't go to school by bus. You know that. We walk together."

"You're missing the point. I'm saying you might have met my father and not known it was him because he's a master of disguise. There was a park near my old house and once I was walking through it and someone called my name. I looked around and at first I thought no one was there. I heard my name again and recognized Dad's voice. He was standing right next to me. He was disguised as a tree."

"A tree?"

"A grapefruit tree," Calvin said, "with lots of grapefruit hanging on its branches."

I don't believe everything Calvin says, but still, since he told me that, I check out the trees whenever I'm in a park.

We're on our way to Clover Street.

"I've been thinking about Mom giving jelly shots at the bakery," Calvin says. "I bet before

31

each shot, she'll tell the donut, 'This won't hurt a bit.' That's what she always told me before I got a shot. She'll say, 'Now be a good little donut,' and, 'This will make you strong and healthy.'"

I say, "I don't think she'll talk to the donuts."

"Oh, yes she will. She'll start out talking about jelly shots. From there she'll talk about gunshots and that she doesn't like watching some television shows because of all the *bang-bang* noises, that she holds her hands over ears when she watches those shows and you have to be careful when you clean your ears."

That *is* how Calvin's mother talks. She goes from one thing to the next. It's fun listening to her.

"Inside each ear is an eardrum," Calvin tells me. "Mom will tell the donuts that. Then she'll talk about how I play the drums and may become a rock musician."

I didn't know Calvin plays the drums.

"You know what Mom will talk about next?"
I shake my head. I don't know.

"From rock music, she'll move on to rocks and maybe even to rock climbing or that a diamond is a rock and that the baseball infield is called a diamond."

"Your mom is fun," I tell Calvin.

We're on Clover Street. Now we look for a small blue house.

There's a big house on the corner with a few trees in the front yard. I check. None of the trees is Mr. Waffle.

There's a small house on the opposite corner, but it's not blue. It's red brick and the grass

needs to be cut. I know it's not Mrs. Cakel's house because she wouldn't allow her grass to grow that long. She probably has a sign on her front lawn with a whole list of rules her grass, bushes, and trees must follow.

We walk slowly down the block and look at all the houses. One is blue-gray, but it's not a really small house and it needs to be painted. We both don't think it's the one.

"There," Calvin says.

He points to a small house that's across the street and near the other end of the block.

"I think that's it," Calvin says.

The house is painted blue. The frames around the windows are white. The front lawn is cut and trimmed. Against the house is a row of those bushes that are always green and they're trimmed into perfect rectangles. On one side is a long gravel driveway.

There's no sign on the front lawn, but I tell Calvin I think he's right.

"What do we do now?" I ask.

"We make sure it's her house."

We slowly walk down the block until we're right across from it.

"There's no car in the driveway and the windows are all closed," Calvin whispers. "Whoever lives in that house is probably not home."

Calvin crosses the street and I follow him. He starts up the walk of the blue house toward the front door.

"Hey! What are you doing?"

"Sh!" Calvin says and holds his pointing finger to his lips.

I follow him, but I'm not happy about walking on someone else's property, especially if it's Mrs. Cakel's.

There's a small painted basket attached to the wall by the front door and it's loaded with mail.

"We're in luck," Calvin says and takes the mail from the basket.

"Put that back," I tell him. "Taking someone else's mail is against the law. You might get us arrested."

"Her name is on the mail. This is where she lives," he tells me, "and her first name is Beatrice. She's Beatrice Cakel."

Calvin looks at the name on each of the letters.

"Every letter is addressed to Beatrice Cakel, so I think she lives alone."

"Put that back and let's get out of here," I tell him.

Calvin looks at me and says, "You would make a lousy spy."

He looks at the mail again.

"There's a news magazine, an electric bill, an advertisement for a new car, and a letter from some place called 'Protect the Animals.' She doesn't like children but I guess she likes animals."

"Put it back."

Calvin puts the mail back in the basket. "Let's just get out of here."

Calvin leaves the front door and walks around the side of the house. I should leave but I don't. I follow him.

Her backyard is neat too. There's a tall white fence around it. The grass is dark green and short, like you'd see on a golf course. In one corner is a large patch of dirt with sticks and on each stick is a sign: Carrots; Cucumbers; Cantaloupe; Casaba Cauliflower.

"Look at that," Calvin says. "She only planted vegetables and melons that begin with the letter C. Cakel begins with C. My name begins with a C. Maybe that's why she likes me so much."

I think he's joking about her liking him.

I wait by the back door as Calvin walks toward the back fence. He walks all along the fence and then returns to me.

"I didn't find anything," he says. "I guess we can go."

37

Crunch! Crunch! Crunch!

What's making that noise?

I look around the side of the house and see an old blue car coming up the driveway. I'm too scared to try and see who's driving it but I'm sure it's Mrs. Cakel.

CRUNCH!

CRUNCH!

CRUNCH!

CRUNCH!

CRUNCH!

CRUNCH!

"We have to get out of here," I tell Calvin.

The fence has us trapped. The only way out of the backyard is the way we came in. We have to walk around the side of the house to the front.

"We can't leave now. She'll see us," Calvin whispers. "We have to hide back here until she goes in."

I look around. There's just grass, the fence, and the vegetable and melon garden that right now is just dirt. There's absolutely no place to hide.

"Where?" I ask.

"Come with me."

He lies down on the grass under one of the windows.

"Even if she looks out, she won't see us." He smiles and says, "You're lucky I'm here."

No, I'm not. If Calvin wasn't here, I wouldn't be lying on the grass and hiding. I would never have even walked up to Mrs. Cakel's front door. I'd be on my way home.

Home!

I look at my watch.

It's already past five. I should be home now cooking spaghetti.

We hear a car door close.

"Next she'll get her mail and go in," Calvin whispers. "Then we can leave."

"Maybe she'll come back here," I whisper. "Maybe she'll check on her vegetables."

We lie there really quiet for what seems a long time. Then we hear a noise from inside the house.

Click!

The noise is right above us. She's about to open the window.

We scoot out real fast. We run along the side of the house, across her front walk, and halfway down the block.

I look back.

No one is following us. I stop by a tree that's between the sidewalk and the street and lean against it.

Calvin leans against the tree and says, "That was fun."

"No. It wasn't fun. It was wrong. And we still don't know why Mrs. Cakel got weird, you know, nice."

I look at my watch.

"I've really got to get home."

I look at Calvin and notice a sign tacked on the tree.

40

"Lost dog. Reward."

Beneath the sign is a picture of a dog and a telephone number.

It's a big tree. Four signs are tacked onto it.

There are lots of trees on this block between the sidewalk and the street. We look at them all. They all have the same Lost Dog signs. Each of the big trees has a few signs.

At the corner we cross the street. There are signs on the next block too, but just one sign on each tree. On the block after that, only some of the trees have signs.

"Do you know what this means?" I ask Calvin.

"Someone lost a dog."

"Whoever put up these signs probably started on Clover Street. As she got farther away, she was running out of signs, so she put fewer up."

"She?"

I tell Calvin, "I think Mrs. Cakel lost her dog."

Just ahead is another tree with a sign. I

get real close and look at the picture of the dog. It's one of those French dogs with fancy haircuts. Beneath the picture it says, "Lost Dog! Reward!" There's a telephone number and then "Dog answers to the name Lollipop."

"No," Calvin says. "This is too funny. Mrs. Cakel's first name is Beatrice and she has a dog named Lollipop with a puffy, froufrou haircut!"

I don't know what froufrou is.

"Maybe I'm wrong," I say. "Maybe it's not her dog."

"I'll find out," Calvin says.

I don't have a cell phone but Calvin does. He takes it out and calls the number on the sign.

He waits.

I hear the muffled sounds of someone answering his call.

Calvin listens for a moment. He presses the Power Off button.

"It's her," Calvin says. "It's Beatrice."

We walk toward home and Calvin says the same thing again and again. He sort of sings it.

"Beatrice lost her Lollipop.

"Beatrice lost her Lollipop.

"Beatrice lost her Lollipop."

It's not good that Calvin found out Mrs. Cakel's first name. Who knows what he might do with that. It's not good, but it's funny when he sings, "Beatrice lost her Lollipop."

I try to keep from smiling, but I can't.

I don't look at Calvin.

I don't want to encourage Calvin Waffle. That's just about the worst thing I could ever do.

PRACTICING   DIRTY   LOOKS

SURPRISED

OTHER   LOOKS

Chapter 4

~~~~~~~~~~~~~~~~~~~~~~~~~~~~~~~~

ROOM FOR
BUTTER PECAN

I think of Karen and that I'm already late for my appointment with the spaghetti pot, and that keeps me from smiling. We're on our way home and I'm walking fast.

Then I tell Calvin, "Some people get really attached to their pets. Mrs. Cakel must really miss Lollipop."

"I know what reward I want," Calvin says. "I want no more homework for the rest of the year. I want to be allowed to chew gum, and slouch, and mumble. Just me. Annie will be so jealous that I'm allowed to chew gum and she's not."

"We haven't found Lollipop."

"We will find that Candy-On-A-Stick dog," Calvin says. "And as a reward, she'll let me sit in the back of the class and play computer games and chew hard candies. Maybe I'll even wear a yellow headband."

I remind Calvin that we're in this together. We'll both look for her dog and I won't do it for the reward.

"That's you," Calvin says. "I'm buying the biggest box of gum I can. I'll buy two. Once we find that Lollipop, I'll be gum chewing and gum popping all day."

We're on our block. We get to my house first.

"We'll start our search tomorrow, right after school," Calvin says. "With my spy training, finding a dog will be easy."

I say good-bye to Calvin. Then I open the front door to my house and walk in.

"Do you know what time it is?" Karen asks.

46

She's holding four dinner plates.

I look at my watch.

"Five thirty."

"Take these," she says and gives me the plates. "Set the table. Make the spaghetti and heat up the sauce. We can't serve it cold."

I put the plates on the dining room table.

I take out a big pot and a small pot, a box of spaghetti, and a can of tomato sauce. I half-fill the big pot with water. I put a few long pieces in the water. I break the others into smaller pieces so they will be easier to eat. I put the spaghetti in the big pot, the pot on the stove, and turn on the burner.

I open a can of sauce, pour it in the smaller pot, put the pot on the stove, and turn on the burner.

Cooking is easy. Maybe I'll become a chef.

"Something is definitely going on," Karen tells me. "Mom came home a while ago. She went right up to her and Dad's room and closed the door."

I finish setting the table.

I turn off the fires under the two pots.

I take the spaghetti to the sink and pour it through a colander. That's a fancy word for a metal bowl with lots of holes. The colander holds onto the spaghetti but lets the water drip out.

Colander is not the only cooking word I know. I know spatula, sauce pan, poach, simmer, consommé, quiche, and confectioner's sugar. I don't know what they all mean, but right now I'm not a chef.

Karen brings her salad to the table. It looks normal, but you have to be careful with any food Karen makes.

I hear the door to Mom and Dad's room open. They're coming down the stairs.

Karen whispers, "Don't talk on and on like you usually do. Let Mom and Dad talk. I'm sure they have something to tell us."

Mom and Dad come into the dining room.

Mom takes her seat at one end of the table. Dad sits at the other end.

"Danny," Mom says. "I know you set the table because there are no napkins."

Karen gives me a dirty look.

Mom says, "If Karen set the table, there would be napkins but no glasses."

I want to give Karen a dirty look, but I'm not sure how to do that.

I once tried to practice making dirty faces with a mirror. It just looked to me like I bit into something that tasted yucky. I decide to practice some more. I'm already ten. At my age, I should be able to give someone a dirty look.

I bring in the big bowl of spaghetti. Karen brings in the salad and the small bowl of sauce.

Mom and Dad each take a large helping of Karen's salad. I watch them taste it.

"Very interesting," Dad says.

Food shouldn't taste interesting. It should taste good.

Very interesting!

"What spices are in here?" Mom asks.

"Ground cumin, ginger, and pepper," Karen says. "Salt is not good for you, so I didn't use any."

Cumin? Ginger? No salad for me!

I finish my first serving of spaghetti and I'm ready for more.

I fish in the bowl for the long pieces. They're fun to eat.

Dad puts down his fork and says, "I have something to tell you."

Here it comes.

"I lost my job. I was fired."

Today my dad lost his job and Mrs. Waffle got one.

Karen asks, "Did you do something wrong?"

Dad shakes his head.

"My boss said I was a great salesman but he's giving my job to his brother-in-law. Mr. Crandel said family comes first."

I tell Dad, "That's so not fair."

Mom says, "I agree, but life is not always fair."

I wonder if my parents will run out of money. Food and clothing are expensive. Mom only works three days a week.

I put my fork down. I'm no longer hungry.

"Dad," Karen asks. "Did you really like selling plumbing things?"

"It's not the plungers I liked. It was the people. As a salesman I spent all day meeting and talking to people. I'm a real people person."

"What's a people person?" I ask. "Aren't all persons people and all people persons?"

"What I mean is, I like to be with people, to work with them."

"Your dad will find something," Mom tells Karen and me. "He's too good a salesman to be out of work for long."

I tell them about Mrs. Waffle's new job.

"Maybe Dad can get a job in her bakery. He could put the sprinkles on cookies or the raisins in the raisin bread."

"We'll see," Dad says.

Mom puts her fork down. I look at her plate. She ate all her spaghetti, but she left a mound of salad.

"Who wants dessert?" Mom asks. "Who wants ice cream?"

I do. There's always room for ice cream, especially butter pecan.

Chapter 5

TWO SHOTS
OF JELLY

It's Tuesday morning.

"Look what I have," Calvin says on our way to school. He shows me a purple lollipop. He shakes his lunch bag. "I have a lot more. I'll give them out."

I shake my head.

"Don't you get it?" Calvin asks. "It will be funny."

"No, it won't," I tell him. "It would be mean. It would just remind Mrs. Cakel of her lost dog."

Calvin takes the wrapper off. "Purple is my

favorite flavor," he says and puts the candy in his mouth.

Calvin takes the lollipop out of his mouth and says, "Lots of people talk to their pets. I know that and I have a lot of questions for Lollipop. I want to know what Mrs. Cakel says about me. I want to know what class she's putting me in for next year."

I think he's joking but I'm not sure. He has some strange ideas.

We're outside the school now and I tell Calvin to finish his lollipop. He pulls it out of his mouth and shows me that there's still a lot left.

ARF! ARF!
"Oh, That Calvin Waffle," Beatrice says. "If I could, I'd send him back to Kindergarten." ARF! ARF!

"You have to finish it," I say. "You can't let Mrs. Cakel see it."

Calvin bites it.

"That's bad for your teeth," I tell him.

"You said I have to finish it and I'm not going to waste a purple," he says and takes another bite.

Sometimes Mrs. Cakel stands by the door to our room and greets us when we walk in, but not today. She's in the room sitting behind her desk and she's slouching. Her slouch tells me she hasn't found Lollipop.

Calvin sits in the front row, and when Mrs. Cakel goes to the board to write something, he takes a lollipop from his pocket and waves it at me. He thinks it's funny.

"What's with the lollipop?" Annie asks him during lunch.

Calvin tells her and Douglas about Mrs. Cakel's dog. He tells them that this afternoon, after we do our homework, we'll start our search for what he calls Mrs. Cakel's Candy-On-A-Stick dog.

"What?" Douglas asks.

"A lollipop is a candy on a stick," Calvin explains.

"I can't go with you," Annie says. "Clover Street is too far from my house."

"I'm getting a swim lesson," Douglas says.

He turns his head and reaches his arms up and moves them like he's swimming right here in the cafeteria.

"Let's eat," Calvin says.

He reaches into his lunch bag and takes out his marshmallow-banana-carrot-on-whole-wheat-bread sandwich.

"Not again!" he complains. "Every day it's the same thing. I hate this stuff."

I tell my friends about Dad.

Douglas asks me, "What's he doing today? It must feel funny to him to stay home."

"This morning he has an appointment with some employment counselor. Maybe he already has a new job."

That's what I say, but I don't really think it will happen so fast.

Calvin takes out a few lollipops.

"Who wants one?"

"I want orange," Douglas says. "Oranges have vitamin C."

"Lollipops are just sugar and artificial flavoring," I tell him.

"What about the stick?" Calvin asks.

"And a stick."

Annie takes a green lollipop and I take a red.

I tell everyone, "We have to finish them before we get back to class. We can't let Mrs. Cakel see our lollipops."

"Mrs. Cakel is not the only one really attached to her pet," Douglas says. "My dad's sister is my Aunt Selma and she has a parakeet. Aunt Selma makes me say, 'Hello, Petey.' So I do it and you know what? Petey never says, 'Hi, Douglas. I'm glad you came to visit.'"

Annie says, "Mrs. Cakel

Hello
Douglas
Hello
Douglas
Hello
Douglas

and your Aunt Selma should get some people friends."

"Lots of people already have all the friends they want," Calvin says. "Along comes someone new and people just ignore him. Maybe they think he's strange. Making friends is not always so easy."

Calvin is talking about himself. When he first came to our school, lots of kids in our class ignored him. Some kids thought he was strange. Some kids still think that. Sometimes I think that, but I like him anyway.

I take the wrapper off my red lollipop and pop it in my mouth.

"Do you know what I think?" Annie asks as she tears the wrapper off her pop.

"You think you'll be the first girl football player in the NFL," Douglas says. "You think you'll be a doctor, electrician, scientist, writer, and cartoonist."

"Yes, and I think green is the best lollipop flavor."

Calvin shakes his head.

"They all taste the same. If I blindfolded you and gave you a pop, you wouldn't know what flavor it was. I like purple because I like the way it makes my tongue look."

Calvin sticks out his tongue. It's purple.

"Once I mixed red and blue food coloring in a soda bottle cap. That made purple. I dipped a Q-tip in and wiped it on my tongue. Then I wiped it on my nose, cheeks, and chin. Mom said I looked like a big grape."

I look around the cafeteria, at all the kids eating and at those waiting on line for more food and drinks. I think about what we do every lunch period when we first get to the cafeteria. We eat. We talk later.

"People like to eat," I tell my friends. "Dogs like to eat too."

"Is my tongue orange?" Douglas asks and sticks out his tongue.

"That's how we'll find Lollipop," I say.

"We'll start out at Mrs. Cakel's house and look for places a dog could find something to eat."

Douglas still has his tongue out.

"It's orange," I tell him.

That afternoon, I don't pay much attention in class. I keep thinking about Lollipop. Meat. That's what dogs eat. Where would a stray dog get meat?

I ask Calvin that on our way home.

"Sometimes people find a lost dog and keep it. Sometimes they don't know whose dog it is."

"Mrs. Cakel put signs up everywhere," I say. "And I'm sure there's a collar around Lollipop's neck. Whoever finds her will know whose dog she is."

We get to our block and Calvin says, "Let's do our homework in my house. This is Mom's first day on her job and I'm sure she brought home some donuts."

His mom left for work really early, like five something in the morning.

"I'm not sure this job will work for her," Calvin tells me. "Mom doesn't like to get up at five in the morning."

Calvin gives me his cell phone. I call home to tell Karen where I'll be and Dad answers the phone.

"Be home by six," Dad tells me. "I'm making hamburgers for dinner."

I wonder how Dad's schedule will change at whatever his new job will be. I wonder if he'll get a new job.

Calvin was right. His mom brought home jelly donuts and lots of other bakery treats. There's a tray of them on the kitchen table.

"Eat something before you do your homework," Mrs. Waffle tells us.

She gives each of us a donut.

"I gave each of them two shots of raspberry jelly," she says. "'This will keep you from getting mumps,' I told the donuts before each shot. 'This will keep you from getting measles.'"

Calvin was right. She talks to the donuts.

The donut she gave me is heavy. It must be all the jelly.

I bite into one end of my donut and red jelly squirts out the other end. It's all over Calvin's shirt. Calvin's donut squirts onto my shirt. Mrs. Waffle wipes our shirts with a paper towel, but instead of cleaning them she spreads the jelly.

"Leave it," Calvin tells her.

"Wait," she says. "I'll put them in the washing machine. I'll clean them super-fast. Meanwhile, you both can wear Calvin's clean shirts."

She hurries to Calvin's room while I unbutton my shirt. She comes back with two T-shirts. On the front of the one she gives Calvin is the picture of a donkey and the message, "Don't get close to me. I kick." On the front of mine it says, "I dunt spel gud."

That's true. Calvin doesn't spell good.

Calvin and I put on the T-shirts.

I take another bite of my donut. Well, not really a bite, more of a nibble. I don't want to get jelly on Calvin's T-shirts.

"It's good," I tell Mrs. Waffle. "It's really good."

"And really messy," she says. "Maybe that's why my boss kept telling me, 'Just one squirt. Just one squirt.'"

We drink some milk, eat some cookies with sprinkles, and eat another donut. I bite into this one over the sink. We also do our homework.

"Mom," Calvin says when we're done. "Danny and I are going out. We're going to look for Lollipop."

"You're still hungry? You can eat candy after all that cake?"

Calvin tells her that Lollipop is the name of Mrs. Cakel's dog and then we leave.

We get to Mrs. Cakel's house and I tell

65

Calvin, "We're two dogs and we're hungry. Where will we go to get something to eat?"

"Ruff! Ruff!"

"I'm serious. Where would a hungry dog go for food?"

"Ruff! Ruff!" Calvin says again.

There is no car in Mrs. Cakel's driveway so we know she's not home. We both stand in front of her house and think.

"The garbage," Calvin says. "Dogs, cats, raccoons, and bears all will eat from garbage pails. Maybe someone on this block has a can with a loose lid."

"I can't imagine the dog on those posters with its poodle haircut eating garbage. I can't

imagine her eating crusts of bread and licking sticky candy wrappers. And if Lollipop was right here, why wouldn't she go home?"

"Maybe she doesn't like Beatrice Cakel," Calvin says. "Nobody really likes that woman."

I shake my head. That's not it.

"There are a bunch of stores near here. I think one of them is a butcher shop. Maybe someone there is feeding her scraps of meat."

"Lead me there," Calvin says. "Ruff! Ruff!"

We walk farther from our block toward the shopping area. There are Lollipop posters on some of the trees, but not as many as there are on Clover Street. I take down one of them and put it in my book bag.

"It's so I can show Lollipop's picture and ask people if they saw her."

We pass the drugstore at the corner.

"Look at that," Calvin says and points to a sign in the drugstore window. "They're selling air conditioners for a dollar. We could use one."

"That's *hair* conditioner."

"Air conditioner, hair conditioner, what's the difference?"

"One keeps you cool and the other nourishes your hair."

As soon as I say it, I feel stupid. I know he didn't think they're selling air conditioners for a dollar.

Of course, with Calvin, I can't be sure.

The third store from the corner is a butcher shop. We look in back. It's clean. There are no meat scraps or open garbage cans.

"Let's go inside," I say. "Maybe they've seen Lollipop. Maybe they're feeding her."

The man behind the counter is cutting meat for a customer. Calvin points to the many red stains on his apron and whispers, "Maybe he ate one of Mom's jelly donuts."

He didn't. The red is blood.

"Can I help you?" the man asks.

"We're looking for a dog."

"I don't sell dog meat."

"We're looking for this dog," I tell him and show him the poster with the picture of Lollipop.

He shakes his head. He hasn't seen her.

I put the poster back in my book bag. The man takes off his apron.

"It's closing time," he says. "It's time for dinner."

Dinner!

I look at my watch. It's six fifteen.

"I've got to get home," I tell Calvin.

"Thanks," I tell the man and hurry out the door.

Chapter 6

EVERYONE KNOWS ABOUT CALVIN

"I'm late again," I tell Calvin.

I'm running home and Calvin has trouble keeping up. I'm pretty fast. Maybe I'll join the track team in high school.

"I'll see you tomorrow," I tell Calvin and hurry into my house.

"You're late," Mom says. "Wash your hands and sit down."

I wash and sit in my seat at the dinner table. Dad gives me a plate with a hamburger on a toasted bun and some fries.

"Where did you get that shirt?" Mom asks. "'I dunt spel gud'!"

"His teacher probably gave it to him," Karen says. "Did you fail another spelling test?"

I forgot I was wearing Calvin's T-shirt.

I tell my parents and Karen about Mrs. Waffle's donuts. I also tell them about our search for Lollipop and our idea to look for places a lost dog would get something to eat.

"It's good of you to look for Mrs. Cakel's dog," Mom says. "Next time let me know if you're going to be late."

"Lollipop!" Karen says. "That dog probably ran off to court to legally change her name."

"I think Danny is right," Mom says. "The dog has to eat, so places that might have leftover meat are good places to look. But you know, the shop you went to is not the only place in town that sells meat. Every supermarket sells meat, and we get our meat two blocks from that store, at the kosher market."

We don't eat ham or anything from a pig. That's not kosher. We also don't eat lobsters, clams, or shrimp.

Dad tells me, "Restaurants sell meat meals and they have lots of leftovers that they throw out."

"Here's a picture of Lollipop," I say and show them the poster. "Let me know if you see her."

"There's a reward for finding the dog," Karen says. "Is that why you're looking for it? Maybe if you find her dog, Mrs. Cakel will promote you to the fifth grade."

Mom says, "Stop teasing your brother. He's a good student."

I put ketchup on my hamburger and bite into it.

Yuck!

I take off the top of the bun and look at what

I'm eating. The meat is burnt on the outside and almost raw inside. I wonder if Lollipop would eat this.

I hope Dad gets a job soon and Mom cooks the hamburgers again.

Dad tells us, "I have two job interviews tomorrow. In the morning I'm going to Malcolm's Breads. They advertised for a salesman, but mostly it's a delivery job. If I get the job, I'd have to get up really early and deliver packaged breads to a whole bunch of stores. The sales part is in the afternoon when I'd make calls and try to get new customers."

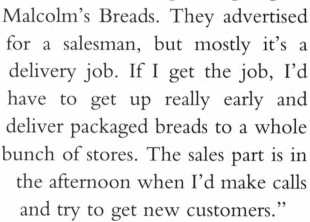

"What's early?" Mom asks.

"Four o'clock."

"You'll have to be quiet," Mom says. "You could leave your clothes in the guest room so you don't wake the rest of us."

"The other job is at a bicycle shop. I'd sell bicycles and exercise equipment. The store doesn't open until ten, so I could get up at a regular time."

I hope Dad gets that job. Maybe they sell unicycles. That's like a bicycle but with just one wheel. I've always wanted to try riding one. I also want to learn to juggle.

The next morning Calvin comes outside with my shirt on a hanger. All the jelly is off. I can't take it to school, so I drop it off at home. Now we have to hurry, or we'll be late.

We get to school just as the bell rings. We'll be late to class, but just by a minute. I expect Mrs. Cakel to be standing by the door to our classroom, but she's not there. Mr. Telfer tells us she's absent. Maybe she's too upset to come to school. Maybe she wants to spend the day looking for Lollipop. Or maybe what Mr. Telfer told us is true. Maybe she's sick.

Our substitute teacher is Mr. Jacobs. He

used to teach here but then he retired. He got old and that's what people do when they get old. Teachers retire because they want to stop going to work and then they keep coming back to the school they worked in.

I don't get it, but I don't get lots of things old people do.

Mr. Jacobs hands out some math worksheets. After we're done with that he wants us to read. He brought along two large baskets of books. I think they're from his class library from when he was a teacher.

There are lots of problems on the worksheets and they're not easy.

The first is multiplication, 37 x 27 = ?

I work slowly. I want to get the right answer.

Hey!

The answer is 999.

Three nines.

How cool is that!

The second problem is multiplication, 37 X 18 = ?

The answer is 666.

Here's a word problem:

A bus is on its way uptown. There are 12 passengers sitting on the right side of the bus. There are 8 passengers sitting on the left side of the bus. No passengers are standing. How many people are on the bus?

It's a trick question. 12 + 8 = 20, so there are 21 people on the bus. There are 20 passengers and 1 bus driver.

"I'm finished," Calvin calls out.

"That's fast," Mr. Jacobs says and takes Calvin's worksheets.

Calvin doesn't really do math. He just makes up answers and writes them down.

Mr. Jacobs tells Calvin to find something to read.

Calvin looks through the two baskets of books.

Mr. Jacobs looks through Calvin's worksheets.

"These are all wrong," Mr. Jacobs tells Calvin. "Mr. Telfer told me there were good students in this class," he says as he puts a large red zero on the top of each of Calvin's worksheets. "I guess he doesn't know about you."

Yes he does. Everyone in school knows about Calvin Waffle.

At lunch we talk about Mr. Jacobs. Everyone thinks he's nice.

"He lets us slouch and get comfortable when we read," Annie says. "I forgot what it's like to have a nice teacher."

I knew Mrs. Cakel wasn't there, but this morning I still sat up. This afternoon I'll try to slouch.

Mr. Jacobs already told us we wouldn't have homework, so after school Calvin and I will drop off our things at home and walk back to town.

Calvin has a bunch of broken cookies from his mom's bakery. He shares them with us.

"They can't sell these," he says, "but cookie pieces taste just as good as whole ones."

He's right.

We read some more after lunch. Then Mr. Jacobs tells us we can talk quietly for the last hour. I feel really relaxed when the school day ends.

I hope Mrs. Cakel is also absent tomorrow.

THE DONUT SPRINKLE MESS

Chapter 7

BEST FRIENDS

We have no homework, so we can get right to our Lollipop hunt. It's exciting to be a lost dog detective. When we find Lollipop, maybe Mrs. Cakel will be so happy and will become warm and loving like my kindergarten teacher, Mrs. Herman.

I don't think so.

On our first day with her as our teacher, we were really noisy. Most of us hadn't seen each other since June. Mrs. Cakel just stood there and looked at her watch. She didn't say a word. She just waited. When we were finally quiet, she told us, "I waited twelve minutes and thirty-six seconds for you. You'll wait that long after the lunch bell rings before I dismiss you." And she did, even the thirty-six seconds.

She's not a screamer but she's strict. She'll never be warm and loving.

"Let's leave our book bags at my house," Calvin says on our way home. "Maybe Mom has some bakery treats for us."

She does.

We walk in and his mother tells us, "I was promoted. I'm now in charge of jelly donut research and development."

Calvin says, "But you were only working there one day."

"Two days."

Mrs. Waffle walks toward the kitchen. Now she turns and says, "Well, come on. You have to help me with my research."

In the kitchen, on the table, is a large plate

of jelly donuts. There's also a container of milk and paper cups.

"A man came into the bakery this morning and he's wearing a suit and tie and the suit is blue with thin white stripes, like he works as a banker or some job that doesn't get his hands dirty. You know, when I bake, my hands get covered with flour and jelly. If my nose tickles and I scratch it, I get flour and jelly on that too. I look like a clown. That must be fun, being a clown, and making people laugh."

"Mom," Calvin says, "what about the man in the suit?"

"Did I tell you about him? He came into the bakery and said that yesterday he bought a jelly donut and it was the best he ever had. He said it was messy, but he liked all the extra jelly. That's when I told my boss that I put two shots in every donut. Now there's a sign in the window advertising our 'Double jelly donuts.'"

Calvin and I sit by the table. His mother gives each of us a paper plate.

"My boss wants me to do donut experiments."

She cuts one donut in small pieces. We each taste it.

"This is my double flavor donut. It's got one shot of raspberry and one shot of apricot."

It's good and that's what I tell Mrs. Waffle.

I take another piece.

She cuts a few more donuts.

The next piece I take has what looks like black jelly. I taste it.

Yuck!

"It's filled with prune butter."

"Not good," I tell Mrs. Waffle.

I need to wash away the prune taste. I pour some milk in a cup and quickly drink it.

The next one is filled with colored candy

84

sprinkles. I bite into it and sprinkles spill all over the table and my pants.

"I like sprinkles on cookies and cake," I tell Mrs. Waffle, "but in a donut, they are kind of dry."

I tell her that of the three, my favorite is the raspberry apricot.

We finish our snack and walk toward Clover Street.

"How could anyone eat a prune donut?" Calvin asks.

"Old people like prunes," I tell him as we walk. "They like toast and tea and boiled chicken and dry cake."

"Maybe that's what made Mrs. Cakel sick," Calvin says. "Maybe she ate too much dry cake. Maybe she's de-something."

"Dehydrated."

"Yeah. Maybe she needs a big drink of water."

We're on Clover Street, across the street from Mrs. Cakel's house. Her car is not in the driveway.

"Maybe she's at her doctor's office being examined," I tell Calvin.

"Maybe she's at the movies," Calvin says, "or in some teacher store buying more workbooks for us to do or at the printer making up a new 'NO' sign with lots more things not to do."

We walk toward town. The lost dog posters are still on the trees, so I'm sure Lollipop is still missing. If she had her dog, Mrs. Cakel would take down the signs.

We walk past the butcher shop to the next block where there's a pizza shop and a restaurant. We walk to the back of both places and look at the garbage. There's a large metal garbage bin behind each store. The lids on them are heavy. We're sure that a small dog couldn't lift them.

"Lollipop wasn't here," I say.

We walk to the next block and Calvin grabs my arm. "Look by the traffic light," he whispers. "There she is."

I look toward the corner and expect to see a

small dog with a fancy haircut. But I don't. I see an old blue car.

"It's Mrs. Cakel," Calvin whispers. "Look how slowly she's driving. She must be looking for her Candy-On-A-Stick dog."

We stand real close to the window of a clothing store. As the old blue car approaches, we turn and face the store. I don't know why, but Calvin doesn't want her to see us.

She drives past.

"We can't let her find her dog," Calvin tells me.

"Why? All that really matters is that someone finds Lollipop."

"No, that's not what matters. All that matters is that you and I find her little dog with the froufrou haircut. I need her to stop thinking of me as the troublemaking kid

who doesn't do his work. I need her to think of me as the hero who found her dog."

"Why don't you just do your work?"

Calvin shakes his head.

"Don't you think I tried that? I sit down by the kitchen table, check my notepad, and open my workbook or whatever to the page she assigned. I look at what she wants us to do and I just can't do it. It's too boring. Sometimes I think my mind is like my mother's conversation. It can't stay on one topic very long."

"One day you'll get a job and have to do whatever the boss says."

"The boss won't tell me to do thirty multiplications. I won't take a job like that. I'll take a job doing something I like. Mom did that. She loves to bake."

I think about Dad.

I hope he gets a job he likes.

I hope he gets a job.

On the next block, we walk behind a

supermarket. The garbage bin is tough to get into. It has a heavy lid that's snapped shut. This can't be where Lollipop is eating.

We go behind a restaurant. It's clean here too, and the garbage bin is closed. We're about to leave when Calvin points to a small bowl by the back door.

"That's a doggy bowl," Calvin says. "Maybe Lollipop doesn't have to dig in the garbage. Maybe someone feeds her."

The bowl is empty.

Calvin asks me for the reward poster and I give it to him. He folds it so only the picture of Lollipop is showing. We walk to the front of the restaurant and go inside.

It's mostly empty. It's too early for people to be eating dinner. We walk past several round tables already set with dishes, glasses, knives, spoons, and forks to the door to the kitchen.

Calvin pushes open the door and calls out, "Is anyone here?"

"I'll be right with you," a woman answers.

We wait a few minutes. Then a tall woman wearing a long white apron comes from somewhere in the kitchen.

"You're a little early," she says. "We begin serving dinner at five."

She looks at her watch.

"Oh, my. That's in just ten minutes."

"We didn't come for dinner. We're looking for this dog," Calvin says and shows her Lollipop's picture.

"Ah, isn't she cute," the woman says and sighs. "She comes here every night."

"YES!" Calvin shouts. "We found her."

HI I'M
NAOMI

He leans close and whispers to me, "My dad will be proud. One day I'll be a great spy like him."

The woman tells us her name is Naomi.

"The dog is not here now," she says. "She comes by much later. Is she yours?"

Calvin says, "She's Beatrice Cakel's dog. She's our teacher."

The way Calvin said that it sounded like Lollipop is our teacher, not Mrs. Cakel. But Naomi understood what he meant. She tells us that a few nights ago she saw Lollipop by the back door.

"That dog looked hungry and she didn't look like she was accustomed to search for her dinner, so I gave her leftovers. Wow, did that dog eat fast! After that, I told my waiters not to throw out large leftover portions of meat. We put it in a bowl by the back door. We get busy here about seven. That's when the dog comes by."

We found Lollipop!

"She's skittish," Naomi says. "Whenever one of us gets near her, she runs away. We couldn't even read her dog tag."

That means we can't get Lollipop and bring her to Mrs. Cakel. We have to bring Mrs. Cakel to Lollipop.

I tell Naomi that we'll be back at seven.

On the way home, I tell Calvin, "We have to call Mrs. Cakel and tell her we may have found her dog."

"Not yet," Calvin says. "First, we have to find out what reward we're getting."

"No," I say and stop walking. "We'll call and tell her what Naomi said. Then at seven o'clock, we'll go with her and hopefully find her Lollipop."

Calvin folds his arms. He squeezes his lips together like he just tasted a lemon. If I had to describe his look, I'd say it was determined. He didn't want to return Mrs. Cakel's dog without getting a great reward.

"What has Beatrice Cakel ever done for me?" he asks.

"She's taught you about adverbs, prepositions, and semicolons. She's taught you about parallel and perpendicular lines, improper fractions, mixed numbers, and volcanoes."

Calvin shakes his head.

"There's a big difference," he says. "I didn't want to know about mixed improper volcanoes and that other stuff, and she really wants her Candy-On-A-Stick dog. She's the one who wrote 'Reward' on the posters."

This time I shake my head.

"When you find something that someone lost, you return it. And if you won't return Lollipop because it's the right thing, do it because we're best friends and it's what I want."

Calvin loses that determined look. He unfolds his arms and asks, "I'm your best friend?"

Best Friends

"Yes."

Calvin's lemon-tasting look has changed to a double-jelly-donut look: all smiley.

"Let's go," I say and we continue our walk home.

I go with him to his house to get my books. Before we go in, we call Mrs. Cakel on Calvin's cell.

"I'll talk," I tell Calvin. "If you talk, you might call her Beatrice."

"Hello."

"This is Danny Cohen."

"Who gave you my number? Why are you calling me at home?"

She sounds angry. She sounds like Mrs. Cakel. I tell her about Lollipop.

Now she sounds like Mr. Jacobs, our substitute teacher, and Mrs. Herman, my kindergarten teacher. She says she'll come before seven with her car and pick Calvin and me up at my house. I tell all that to Calvin.

94

Before I leave, Calvin asks, "We can take a reward if she wants to give us one, can't we?"

"Yes."

"Hm," Calvin says. "I wonder what it will be."

Chapter 8

DAD'S GOOD NEWS

"Dad has good news," Karen tells me when I walk in the house.

"What?"

"I don't know," Karen says. "He said he'll tell us at dinner."

"I have good news too."

I tell Karen about Lollipop.

"So now your mean teacher who was nice for a few days will become mean again."

When Karen put it like that, finding Lollipop didn't sound like such good news.

Dad made vegetable soup for dinner and it

tastes like vegetable soup. That's the first good news. Then Dad tells us about the bicycle shop.

"The owner called this afternoon. He said he's been looking for a while for someone to help him. He liked that I seemed to know a lot about bicycles and that I have lots of selling experience. He offered me a job and I accepted. I start Monday."

"That's great," Karen and I say.

Mom just smiles. I think she knew the news before dinner.

"Do you know why he thinks I know about bicycles?"

That's one of those rhetorical questions, the kind you don't answer.

"Before I went to his shop, I checked on the Internet what he sells. Then I researched. I read all about the bicycles and the exercise equipment."

I ask about unicycles and Dad says the store has one or two for sale. He'll let me try riding one, but not right away. Maybe in two or three weeks, he says, after he's been on the job for a while.

I tell Mom and Dad about Lollipop, that Calvin is coming here, and Mrs. Cakel will be picking us up. You want to hear something funny?

That's another rhetorical question. Don't answer it. I'll tell you what's funny.

When I mentioned Mrs. Cakel's name, Dad sat up. He won't even slouch when I talk about her.

"You'll open the door for her," Mom says.

"If I do, she'll think I want to talk about your schoolwork, and this is not about that."

I bet Mom will hide in the kitchen or upstairs. I don't think she or Dad want to see my teacher.

After dinner, I'm about to sit down and do my homework when I remember I don't have any. I take out my doodle book. It's like a regular notebook only I don't do work in it. I doodle.

I draw lots of dog doodles.

Calvin comes by at six thirty. As soon as he's inside, he opens his mouth and shows me a huge wad of gum.

"It's a whole pack," he says. "She can't tell me to spit it out. This isn't school."

Ten minutes later, there's a loud knock on our front door.

Mom and Dad hurry into the kitchen.

I look through the peephole. Dad has told me

100

to never open the door until I know who's out there. It's her. It's hard to describe her look. It's not happy. It's not mean. I guess she's not sure we found her dog.

I open the door.

"Let's go," she says. "I don't want to miss my Lollipop."

Calvin and I sit in the back of her car.

"Buckle up," she tells us and we do.

Calvin opens his mouth really wide and closes it so his teeth make a loud clicking sound. He wants to be sure Mrs. Cakel knows he is chewing. He slouches so much in his seat that he's really sitting on his back and not his backside.

Calvin and I both forgot to look at the name of Naomi's restaurant, but I remember where it is, so I tell Mrs. Cakel where to drive.

Mrs. Cakel stops the car at a red light.

Calvin sits up. He stops chewing his gum.

"Did you ever think why your dog ran away and never came back?" he asks.

She turns and gives Calvin the same look she often gives him in school, like she wishes *he* would run away.

"I was bringing in groceries and left the front door open. She ran out. She must have run to the park. She loves it there. But the park has lots of entrances and I guess she got lost. I never take her to town, so if somehow she got there, she wouldn't know how to get home. I just take her to the park."

The light changes to green and Mrs. Cakel drives ahead.

Calvin is still sitting forward. He's about to say something. I touch his hand and shake my head and he sits back. He's chewing again.

I'm glad he didn't say anything else or call her Beatrice.

"There it is," I say and point to the restaurant.

Mrs. Cakel parks her car. We go inside and I introduce her to Naomi.

"People are just sitting down to eat," Naomi

says. "When they're done, I've instructed my waiters to take any large leftover pieces of meat and put it in the bowl outside. That's where you should wait or you might miss her. Your dog doesn't stay long."

Mrs. Cakel thanks her.

Naomi sets a small bench by the back door. We sit there and wait.

"If we find Lollipop, I'll have you to thank," Mrs. Cakel tells us.

That's all she says. She's not good at what Mom calls small talk.

That's like when people ask, "How are you?" Mom says that's small talk because they don't really want to know how you are.

Once Aunt Ella asked me that and I told her, "I have an itchy toe and I'm having trouble in school with fractions and I can catch ground balls but I can't throw the ball all the way to first base."

Mom said I told Aunt Ella too much. When she asked how I was, I should have just answered that I'm fine.

Well, Mrs. Cakel isn't good with small talk. She doesn't say anything and neither do we. We just sit there.

The back door opens. A waiter scrapes a plate of leftover meat into the bowl.

We wait some more.

The door opens again and another waiter scrapes leftovers into the bowl.

We hear something. We turn. It's Lollipop.

I look at Mrs. Cakel.

Wow!

What a smile! I've never seen her smile like that. It changes her whole face. She even looks nice.

Mrs. Cakel holds out her arms, grabs Lollipop, and says, "Come to me, baby."

The small dog licks her face.

"I missed you."

. Lollipop didn't say that. Mrs. Cakel did.

Calvin and I watch our teacher hug and kiss her pet. It's nice to know she can be like that.

Calvin whispers, "That Candy-On-A-Stick dog doesn't want her kisses. She's hungry."

He's right. While Mrs. Cakel is hugging, her dog is looking at the bowl of meat.

"Lollipop is hungry," I say.

"Are you?" Mrs. Cakel asks Lollipop. "Do you want to eat? Do you?"

Lollipop doesn't answer. She seems to know that's a rhetorical question.

Mrs. Cakel sets Lollipop down and the dog goes right to the bowl. She eats really fast. She licks the bowl when she's done.

Mrs. Cakel picks up her pet. She opens the back door of the restaurant and asks for Naomi.

"This is my baby, my Lollipop," she tells Naomi. "Thank you so much for feeding her."

"You're quite welcome."

"I want to give you something."

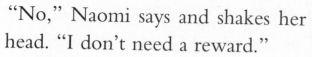

"No," Naomi says and shakes her head. "I don't need a reward."

Mrs. Cakel thanks her again and we walk to her car.

"But I need a reward," Calvin whispers.

Lollipop sits in the front seat and we sit in the back. During the ride, Mrs. Cakel tells Lollipop how much she missed her, how much she loves her, and how many treats she has waiting for her when they get home.

She stops in front of my house. She turns and tells us, "I haven't forgotten about you. You found my baby and I did promise a reward to whoever finds Lollipop. I'll bring your rewards to school tomorrow."

"What are you giving us?" Calvin asks. "We spent three days looking for your dog. It took real good spy work to find her."

"When I wrote 'Reward' on my poster, I planned to give a financial reward."

That's money.

"I didn't know that two of my students would find Lollipop. I can't give my students money. But I'll give each of you a good reward."

"Thank you," Calvin and I say and get out of the car.

"I wonder what she'll give us," Calvin says as he leaves me to go home.

I wonder too.

Chapter 9

A REAL GREAT WEEK

It's Thursday morning.

"She's giving us something she already has," Calvin tells me on our way to school.

"What?"

"It was too late last night for Beatrice to go out and buy rewards, so she's giving us something she had in her house."

I hadn't thought of that.

"She once took a whole bunch of baseball cards from Douglas because he was looking at them in class," Calvin says. "Maybe that's what she's giving us."

I say, "If she gives us those cards, we'll return them to Douglas."

"Maybe she'll give us all the hard candies and cans of soda she's taken from her students."

Calvin must have thought about this a lot.

"Not just the baseball cards, candies, and sodas from this year, but from all her years of teaching."

I tell Calvin, "If you keep soda too long it loses its bubbles. Don't drink from any can that's rusted or dusty."

We meet Douglas and Annie in the school playground. We tell them how we found Lollipop.

"Maybe she baked cookies for you," Annie says. "I bet she's really good at measuring ingredients and following recipes."

I don't need Mrs. Cakel's cookies. I like the cookies and donuts Mrs. Waffle gives me.

The bell rings. We line up and go in the building.

Mrs. Cakel is standing by the door to our room. She has her usual strict look, the same "just-start-something-and-see-what-happens" look she's had all year.

Calvin and I walk past and she smiles.

"I have something for each of you," she whispers. "I'll give it to you at lunchtime."

I look on her desk. Nothing. I wonder what she has for me.

I sit in my seat and try to pay attention but today it's not easy.

The morning lessons go on and on.

George Washington did this. Samuel Adams did this. One-half is more than one-third. Heart. Lungs. Circulatory

111

system. Red blood cells. White blood cells. Platelets. Plasma.

Did you know the heart is a pump? Only you can't use it to fill your bicycle tires with air. Your heart pumps blood all over your body.

The bell!

Lunchtime.

Douglas, Annie, and all the other kids in my class grab their lunches and rush out of the room. Calvin and I don't rush. We're the last ones by the door.

"Here," Mrs. Cakel says and gives me a wrapped package. "This is your reward."

The package is heavy. I tear off the wrapping. She gave me five books. But not just any books—baseball books.

"Danny, I know that you love baseball, so I thought these books would be a good reward."

"Yes, I love baseball. This is a *great* reward."

"And Calvin," she says. "You love to chew gum, to slouch, and to give strange answers in class. I hope you like this reward."

She gives Calvin an envelope.

"Money?" Calvin asks in a whisper.

He carefully opens the envelope and takes out several white cards. Each has a fancy printed border. Inside each border in large bold print are the words "Get Out of Trouble Free." Each card is signed *B. Cakel*.

"There are lots of rules in my classroom," Mrs. Cakel tells Calvin, "and you have trouble following rules. There are seven cards, so seven times during the rest of the school year, if I catch you chewing gum or mumbling, or even without your homework, and you're about to get in trouble, just give me one of those cards. You'll get out of trouble free."

Mrs. Cakel smiles.

"This is great!" Calvin says.

"Thank you for finding my Lollipop," Mrs. Cakel tells us. "Now go eat your lunches."

"This has been a real great week," Calvin tells me on our way to the cafeteria. "It was fun hunting for that Candy-On–A-Stick dog. I got to eat lots of donuts. These Get Out of Trouble Free cards might get me through fourth grade. And best of all, I found out I'm your best friend."

"And the week is not over," I tell my best friend. "It's only Thursday."

Read on for a
sneak peek at

DANNY'S DOODLES

The Dog Biscuit Breakfast

Chapter 1

"Look at that man," my friend Calvin Waffle says.

We're walking to school and Calvin points to a man walking a dog. He's wearing a bathrobe and slippers. That's what the man is wearing, not the dog. The dog is wearing a leash and a collar and has lots of short curly hair.

"I know all about that man," Calvin says.

Maybe he does. Calvin has told me his father is a spy. Maybe Calvin is a spy, too. Maybe he's spied on Bathrobe Man. Maybe he's spied on lots of people in our neighborhood.

Maybe he's been spying on me!

"That man has a child, probably a son named Devon who wanted a dog. 'I'll take care of him,' Devon promised. 'I'll even clean up after him. Please, Dad, please.'"

Calvin stops. He grabs my arm and asks, "And do you know what that man did?"

I shake my head. I don't know. I'm not the spy. Calvin is.

"He bought the dog for his son. Because of all that curly hair Devon named the dog Parsley and for the first two weeks he walked Parsley five times a day. He fed the dog so much that it puked."

"Yuch!"

"That was just two weeks ago and do you know what?"

I shake my head again. How should I know what? I didn't even know the boy's name was Devon.

"Now Devon doesn't even look at Parsley. He surely doesn't take care of him."

120

This is all very interesting but we have to get to school.

"We've got to get going," I tell Calvin. "We can't be late again."

Our teacher is Mrs. Cakel and she doesn't like it when we're late. She doesn't like it if we write our names too small at the top of our homework papers or too big. She doesn't like it when we answer her questions too loud or too low—even if the answer is right. She also doesn't like it if we wear shirts with sparkles or sneakers with blinking lights. Actually, sweet Mrs. Cakel doesn't like most things we do or wear. I don't think she's a happy woman.

Calvin lets go of my arm. We walk toward the corner.

Calvin turns and says, "Now look at him."

I look at Bathrobe Man again. He's pulling on Parsley's leash. The dog wants to smell the grass and Bathrobe Man is in a rush. He looks tired and grumpy. It's Bathrobe Man who looks grumpy, not Parsley.

"Devon no longer wants Parsley," Calvin tells me. "Now he wants a football."

We stop at the corner and wait for the cars to go past.

"Now it's Devon's father who feeds the dog. He walks him. He cleans up after him. Bathrobe Man shouldn't have bought his son a dog. He should have rented one."

"You can't rent a dog," I say.

"Why not? You can rent ice skates, boats, chairs for a party, penguin suits, and cars. Why can't you rent a dog?"

"Penguin suits?"

"Tuxedos. You know, the suits men wear to their weddings." Calvin thinks for a moment and then tells me, "One day I might get married, but I won't wear a tuxedo."

We watch as Parsley lifts one of its back legs. I don't want to say what he does, only that I'll be real careful this afternoon when we walk home from school. I don't want to step where Parsley stopped and did what he did. I'm wearing sneakers and it not easy getting that stuff out of the grooves in the bottoms of sneakers.

Calvin says, "Can you imagine: I'm getting married and I'm wearing the shiny shoes people wear with tuxedos and I step in that stuff. People would smell me as I walk down the aisle."

I can't imagine that. I can't imagine Calvin getting married.

I look at my watch again and say, "We've really got to get going."

He doesn't care if Mrs. Cakel yells, but I do. We cross the street.

As we walk, Calvin keeps talking about Parsley and it's making me hungry. Mom usually serves parsley on fried fish and she serves fried fish with french fries and I love those fries dipped in ketchup.

"We're here," Calvin tells me.

We are. We're in the school playground and we're on time. Kids are still here waiting for the bell to ring.

My friends Douglas and Annie are right by the door. They're not in a hurry to see Mrs. Cakel. It's just that she gives so much homework and we have to take so many books back and forth to school that our book bags are really heavy. They're in a hurry to put their book bags down.

The bell rings.

"I'm going to think about that," Calvin says as we walk into school. "I'm going to think about Devon and his father and that curly-haired dog. I'm going to think about how I can start a rent-a-pet business."

He can't. His mother won't let him have a dog. I think she's allergic.

"There's work on the board," Mrs. Cakel tells us as we walk into class. "Get started."

The whole board is covered with writing. The heading is "Chronology of the Revolution." Under that is a list of years and things that happened in the time of George Washington.

Did you know that Paul Revere and William Dawes were not the only ones to warn that "the British are coming"? That was in 1775. Two years later, in 1777, Sybil Ludington, a sixteen-year-old girl, warned that the British were attacking in Danbury, Connecticut. Sybil Ludington rode eighty miles on a horse named Star.

"Mrs. Cakel could just print off the stuff and give it to us, but she writes it on the board and makes us copy it," Douglas once said during lunch. "She does that to keep us busy and quiet."

"No," Annie said. "Copying that stuff helps us remember it."

I don't try to know why Mrs. Cakel tells us to do things. I just do them. That keeps me out of trouble.

BANG!

Calvin drops his book bag on the floor.

PLOP!

He plops into his seat.

Mrs. Cakel looks at him and it's not an "I'm so glad you're on time today" look. It's more of an "I'll get you" and a "you'll be sorry" look.

I once asked Calvin why he makes so much noise when he comes to class.

"She has a big NO sign in the room," he told me. "No talking in class without permission. No mumbling. No calling out. No walking about. No slouching. No gum chewing. No eating in class. No note sending. It does not say 'No book dropping.' It does not say 'No seat plopping.' That means it's allowed."

"No it doesn't," I told Calvin. "It doesn't say 'No kite flying,' but that doesn't mean you can bring in a kite with lots of string and fly it in the classroom."

"Kite flying in Cakel's class," Calvin said. "That's a great idea."

If anyone else had said that I would know he was joking, but with Calvin, you never know.

"I'll need a breeze," Calvin said, "so I'll open all the windows. I'll get a dragon kite with long paper teeth and a long paper tail." He thought for a moment and then added, "I'll start it flying in the classroom and when it hits the ceiling I'll push it out the window. I'll tie the end of the string to my desk. Oh, this will be fun!"

I didn't tell Calvin he wouldn't be allowed to fly a kite in class. It's not a good idea to tell Calvin what's not allowed. He thinks of the word "no" as a challenge. That might be why he has so much trouble with Mrs. Cakel. She's always telling us what not to do and he's always doing it.

So far, he hasn't brought a kite to class. But the school year is not over.

After we copy the chronology, Mrs. Cakel talks to us about the war. She tells us about the winter beginning at the end of 1777. George

Washington led his troops to Valley Forge, Pennsylvania. It was real cold and many of his soldiers had no coats or shoes. But they worked like beavers—seriously, like beavers—and built cabins with logs and mud. Washington's wife Martha knitted socks for the men. It's too bad she didn't knit shoes and coats for them.

After the Revolution lesson she teaches us more stuff about fractions. Then we read.

Every few minutes while I'm reading, I look at Calvin. He has his book open but I can tell he isn't reading. His eyes aren't moving. Try it. You can't read without moving your eyes.

On our way to lunch Calvin says, "I've been thinking about Devon and Parsley. I can't have a dog or any pet, but I have figured how I can start a rent-a-pet business."

His idea must have something to do with computers. I bet he's going to create virtual pets. It will be just like you have a pet dog, but it will just be on the computer. His idea won't work. A computer can't run to you and wag its tail when you get home from school. You can't pet a computer.

Calvin hasn't told me his idea, just that he has one. I don't know what he's planning, but I think it will lead to trouble. Calvin's ideas usually do.

And don't miss the book
that started it all...

DANNY'S DOODLES

The Jelly Bean Experiment

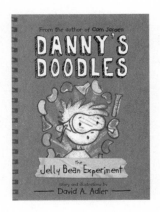

Here's a fact:
My new friend Calvin Waffle is 100% Weird

Danny Cohen and Calvin Waffle are two very different kids. Danny likes playing baseball; Calvin enjoys strange experiments. Danny follows the rules at school; Calvin tries to drive his teacher crazy.

Danny and Calvin decide to team up for the big jelly bean experiment. Will it lead to trouble? Maybe. Will they have fun trying? You can count on it.

ABOUT THE AUTHOR

David A. Adler is a former math teacher, author of the Cam Jansen and Young Cam Jansen series, *Don't Talk to Me About the War,* numerous biographies, math, and science books, and books on the Holocaust. He lives in New York with his wife and family.